PENELOPE
PIG

Nettlepatch Farm

Nettlepatch Farm

PENELOPE PIG

Abigail Pizer

JAMES PRENDERGAST LIBRARY ASSOCIATION

02771289

Carolrhoda Books, Inc.
Minneapolis

This edition first published 1989 by Carolrhoda Books, Inc.

Original edition copyright © 1988 by Abigail Pizer.
Original edition published 1988 by Macmillan Children's Books, a division of
Macmillan Publishers Limited, London and Basingstoke.

All rights reserved.

Library of Congress Cataloging-in-Publication Data

Pizer, Abigail.
    Penelope pig.
    (Nettlepatch farm)
    Summary: Tired of living in a sty and wallowing in the
mud, a young pig tries to move into the Potters' farmhouse.
    1. Swine—Juvenile fiction. [1. Pigs—Fiction.
2. Farm life—Fiction.] I. Title. II. Series: Pizer,
Abigail. Nettlepatch farm.
PZ10.3.P419Pe   1989   [E]   88-34163
ISBN 0-87614-366-4 (lib. bdg.)

Manufactured in the United States of America

1 2 3 4 5 6 7 8 9 10 99 98 97 96 95 94 93 92 91 90 89

It is wintertime at Nettlepatch Farm.
On the farm live Mr. Potter, Mrs. Potter,
their little daughter, Amy, . . .

...and Penelope Pig.

She is fat and pink, with black patches, two large floppy ears, a turned-up nose, and a corkscrew tail.

She lives in a sty with the other pigs.

Penelope may look like the other pigs on the farm, but she doesn't always behave like them.

She doesn't wallow in the mud of the farmyard, and she won't get her nose muddy looking for food.

What Penelope really wants is to live
in the farmhouse. Every day she looks
through the living room window. She
always sees Billingsgate the cat curled
up, warm and comfortable on the sofa.

One cold and frosty morning Penelope follows Billingsgate—around the corner of the barn, across the farmyard, and up to the back door.

The door is ajar, and Billingsgate slips through.

Penelope watches from a distance.

She looks this way. She looks that way.
Nobody is around.
Quickly she trots over to the open door.

She pokes her head in and peers around.
How warm and inviting the house looks!

So in she goes. But where is
Billingsgate? She trots across the
kitchen, leaving muddy hoofprints on
the shiny tiles.

Penelope goes through the doorway,
across the hall, through another
doorway...

...and there is Billingsgate, fast asleep on the sofa.

Penelope climbs right up to join him. Billingsgate doesn't like this at all, but Penelope is very happy.

Just at that moment, Mrs. Potter and Amy return. The first thing they see is Billingsgate running out the back door. Muddy hoofprints lead them through the kitchen, across the hall, into the living room, and there on the sofa is …

"Out!" shouts Mrs. Potter to Penelope.

Penelope jumps off the sofa. Mrs. Potter shoos her toward the door. Amy thinks this is a great game. Poor Penelope is chased across the hall, through the kitchen, and...

. . . out the back door.

Bang! The door slams shut behind her.

Later that day Penelope follows
Billingsgate to the back door again.
The door is still shut, but Billingsgate
has another way of getting in. Penelope
watches him . . .

...and tries the same thing. In goes her head, but the rest of her just won't follow. She tries to pull her head out, but she can't. She's stuck!

Penelope struggles and squeals.
She makes such a noise that Mr. Potter,
Mrs. Potter, Amy, and old Joe the
farmhand all come running.

"There's only one way to tackle this,"
Mr. Potter says. They pull and push,
until...

...plop!
Out comes Penelope, and Mr. Potter,
Mrs. Potter, Amy, and old Joe all fall
over backward into the muddy yard.

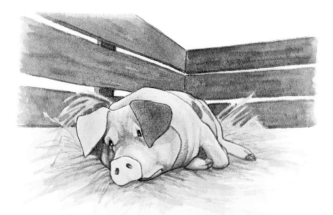

Mr. Potter is very cross.
He sends Penelope back to the sty with
the other pigs, and he tells her never
to come near the house again.
Penelope is sad.
She still wants to sleep on the sofa like
Billingsgate.

But Mr. Potter is not cross for long.
The next day, when he comes back from the
market, there is something special in the back
of his truck.

It's just what Penelope wants!
Now she can be just like Billingsgate.

Nettlepatch Farm

About the Author

Abigail Pizer studied at the Harrow School of Art in Harrow, England, and has a degree in illustration. Since leaving college in 1982, she has worked as a freelance illustrator. In addition to the Nettlepatch Farm books, she is the author and illustrator of *Harry's Night Out* and *Nosey Gilbert*. As a great animal lover, she writes most of her books about animals.

E
Pizer, Abigail.
   Penelope pig

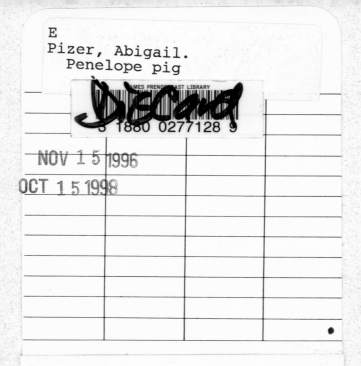

JAMES PRENDERGAST LIBRARY

DISCARD

3 1880 0277128 9

NOV 1 5 1996

OCT 1 5 1998

JAMES PRENDERGAST
LIBRARY ASSOCIATION

JAMESTOWN, NEW YORK

Member Of

Chautauqua-Cattaraugus Library System

5/90